"I have summoned you, the knights who battled the terrible lizards, the bravest knights of the Round Table. I have a task for you," continued Morgause. "The creatures of nightmare are loose in the mist and darkness. They are coming. For you."

"Coming for us?" scoffed Bors. "Fine!

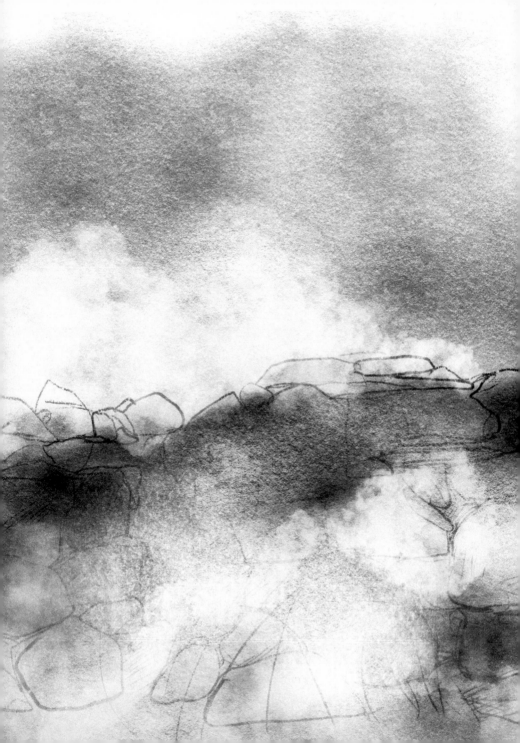

MATT PHELAN

KNIGHTS
vs.
MONSTERS

GREENWILLOW BOOKS
An Imprint of HarperCollinsPublishers

Knights vs. Monsters
Text and illustrations copyright © 2019 by Matt Phelan
First published in 2019 in hardcover by Greenwillow Books; first paperback edition, 2020
All rights reserved. No part of this book may be used or reproduced in any manner whatsoever without written permission except in the case of brief quotations embodied in critical articles and reviews. Printed in the United States of America. For information address HarperCollins Children's Books, a division of HarperCollins Publishers, 195 Broadway, New York, NY 10007.
www.harpercollinschildrens.com

The text of this book is set in Iowan Old Style.
Book design by Sylvie Le Floc'h

Library of Congress Cataloging-in-Publication Data

Names: Phelan, Matt, author, illustrator.
Title: Knights vs. monsters / written and illustrated by Matt Phelan.
Other titles: Knights versus monsters
   Description: First edition. | New York, NY : Greenwillow Books, an imprint of
   HarperCollins Publishers, [2019] | Summary: Yearning for adventure, the young Knights
   of the Round Table are drawn to Orkney, Scotland, where they face a kraken and other
   monsters, including Queen Margause and her son, Mordred.
Identifiers: LCCN 2017052114 (print) | LCCN 2018049661 (ebook) | ISBN
   9780062686275 (paperback)
Subjects: | CYAC: Knights and knighthood—Fiction. | Monsters—Fiction. |
   Adventure and adventurers—Fiction. | Characters in literature—Fiction. |
   Great Britain—History—To 1066—Fiction. | Humorous stories.
Classification: LCC PZ7.P44882 Knm 2019 (ebook) | LCC PZ7.S96568 (print) |
   DDC [Fic]—dc23
LC record available at https://lccn.loc.gov/2017052114

20 21 22 23 24 PC/LSCH 10 9 8 7 6 5 4 3 2 1
First Edition

 Greenwillow Books

FOR NORA

CONTENTS

PROLOGUE

Something lurked in the mist. Something large. Something nasty.

Four knights and one young girl stumbled half blind on the dark, misty moor as well.

"Where is it?" yelled Sir Erec of the Round Table, brandishing his broadsword. "BORS!"

Sir Bors bounded out of the mist, swinging his sword every which way. "There's more than one! Where's Hector?"

"I don't know. Can't see anything in this blasted mist." Erec turned sharply. "There! I think—"

He didn't finish the sentence. An enormous hairy arm with fiendish claws burst from the mist and sliced Erec's garment.

Bors raised his blade with a deep battle cry. Erec regained his footing and joined the battle.

"Hector! We need you! NOW!" he called.

Elsewhere . . .

Magdalena, the Black Knight, moved slowly, cautiously, a sword in one hand, a dagger in the other. Her eyes, intense and piercing, scanned the impenetrable fog.

She took a single breath.

An enormous tentacle whipped through the mist and wrapped around her legs, knocking her to the ground. She dropped her sword but still held the knife. The Black Knight slashed at the tentacle but could not quite reach it.

The tentacle dragged her across the rocky terrain. A low growl rumbled louder and louder.

Suddenly . . .

An arrow pierced the tentacle. The mysterious beast roared.

Melancholy Postlethwaite leaped from behind a stone wall, a bow in hand, a fresh arrow released in midair.

Mel landed, rolled, sprang to her feet, and helped the Black Knight untangle from the flailing tentacle. But seven more whipped furiously above them. The Black Knight found her sword, drew herself to her full intimidating height, and wiped a strand of hair from her eyes. Mel stood beside her, bow at the ready.

Meanwhile . . .

Bors and Erec soared backward through the air and landed with a thud against a small stone hut.

Winded, they slowly rallied their strength.

The sound of enormous feet crunched toward them.

They froze, eyes on the dark mist. A monster emerged from the gloom. It was huge, terrifying, fierce, and—

"Wait," said Erec. "Is that a wee mustache?"

In a darkened hall of Camelot, two court minstrels sat by a small fire, tuning their instruments.

"That's not it," said the first. "He shouted: 'We must act!'"

"No, it was 'wee mustache.'"

"That doesn't make any sense."

The minstrel shrugged. "That's the most reliable tale at the moment. Some Scottish peasant came through town the other day. He'd heard the tale from a cousin of a cousin who was there and sent a letter all about it via raven. I heard it from John Muddle, the tinsmith. Who told you?"

"Bertha, the innkeeper. But that's exactly the problem, you see. It's all hearsay. Worse, it's whisper-down-the-lane. How is a respectable minstrel expected to know all the little details?"

"We do what we can, Paul."

They continued tuning.

"I hear the squire is now quite an accomplished archer."

"Well, that's what I mean, John. You *hear*? From whom?"

"Lionel. Lutist from . . . Devon, I think."

"Ugh. What a hack."

"I know. But he has a new song called 'Melancholy the Erstwhile Squire Who Is Now an Accomplished Archer.'"

"Good title. But Lionel has no sense of melody."

"Tell me about it. And how difficult is basic song structure? Verse, verse, verse, verse, verse, verse, verse, chorus, repeat."

The fire crackled. A string twanged into tune.

"I wonder where he heard the archer bit."

"Who knows? We won't have the full accurate account, the *actual* facts of the story, until the Band of the Terrible Lizards returns."

"They shan't return."

A dark figure emerged from the shadows of the hall.

"Sir Gawain. We did not see you there."

Gawain stood by the fire and poked it slowly. "I have just received word from my brother, Sir Agravaine. Grave news from our home." Gawain put the poker down and stared at the blazing fire for a moment. "The Band of the Terrible Lizards has met their end. They fought bravely, of course. . . ."

He turned and walked to the door of the hall.

"But some things are unconquerable, even for the greatest of heroes."

CHAPTER ONE

ALWAYS BOARD
A MAGIC BOAT

One week earlier . . .

Sir Erec lifted the grail to the light of the candle. He turned it gently, slowly.

An elderly couple stood a few feet away in the dark cottage. They watched Erec with bated breath.

Erec held the grail still. He examined a detail for a long moment.

"No." Erec tossed the grail casually to his left hand and set it down on the table.

"What do you mean, Sir Erec?" the aged man asked.

"It is surely the Holy Grail you seek."

"It's a nice grail, truly. Great grail. But it's not *the* grail."

"How can you tell?" demanded the lady.

Erec turned by the door.

"Because it doesn't . . . glow or shimmer or . . . vibrate slightly. I'll know it when I see it."

Sir Bors leaned against the door. He rolled his eyes and huffed as Erec walked past him. Bors followed Erec outside the cottage.

"What a surprise," said Bors. "I'm utterly shocked."

"I feel the same as you, Bors. You can save your sarcasm."

"Sarcasm and disappointment are the only things I've gained from this so-called adventure," grumbled Bors.

"Well, King Arthur wants to find the Holy Grail, so on we search."

"Along with every other Knight of the Round Table, including the most pathetic ones."

Erec stopped and faced Bors.

"Are you suggesting we are above the other knights of Arthur's Round Table?"

Bors stepped closer and leaned into Erec.

"We fought the mightiest creatures in history. Face-to-face, sword to tooth. The terrible lizards. And we were victorious. Yes, Sir Erec, I do believe we are above the other knights. We are meant for bigger things."

Erec held Bors's gaze. He sighed.

"I agree."

A hundred yards away, Mel was carefully taking aim with her bow. Magdalena, the Black Knight, stood by her side.

"Take a moment. Hold your breath. See only the target. Forget the bow, the arrow, and everything else around you."

Mel concentrated. She held her breath. She released the arrow. It soared straight and true, hitting a two-inch knot on a thin tree branch.

"Good," said Magdalena.

Mel rolled her head from shoulder to shoulder. "Thank you."

She started to string another arrow, then paused and turned to the Black Knight.

"Thank you for everything, Magdalena. The training, the skills you have taught me."

"Thank yourself. You did the work."

Mel smiled. "Yes, but . . . thank you for believing I *could* do the work. For believing that I could be more than a squire. I never would have dreamed I could be an archer, let alone a full member of this company."

Magdalena looked up into the sky, watching a bird soar overhead.

"It was not such a great leap. You were an exceptionally skilled squire with a keen instinct, Mel. Moreover, you demonstrated great intelligence and stealth, posing as a boy to conceal your identity for so long."

Magdalena glanced across the field as Erec and Bors made their way from the small hut. Bors stepped in a pile of manure, muttered something, and dragged his foot along the grass for a bit.

"Even if it was mostly Bors who you were fooling," said Magdalena.

Mel laughed.

"Yes, I suppose that was not as challenging as it might have been. However," Mel continued, "whether you want to hear it or not, I owe you a great deal, Magdalena. I was not meant to be a squire. Perhaps now I'm becoming what I was always destined to be."

Magdalena turned and walked after Erec and Bors.

"I do not believe in destiny, Mel. Good or bad."

Erec and Bors followed the path through the gate, past a row of bushes, and down to the bank of a wide river. Sir Hector was sitting at the edge of the water, knife in hand, observing his reflection in the water.

"Was it the Holy Grail?" Hector asked as the two approached.

"No. Not even a little bit," said Erec.

"Can't say I'm surprised, fellow knights. Every day it's the same thing. I suppose tomorrow it will be my turn to inspect the local cupboards. Anyhoo . . ."

Hector stood and faced the knights with a beaming smile.

"Notice anything?"

"It's a river," said Bors. "We knew that already."

"No," said Hector. "Notice anything about *me*?"

"I try not to," said Bors, sitting on a rock.

"New tunic?" asked Erec.

"No."

"Weight gain?"

"No!"

Hector twitched his lips and flared his nostrils.

"You shaved your mustache off," said Erec.

"Not off," said Hector petulantly. "It's still there. It's less ostentatious. It's rather dashing now, don't you think?"

"Dashing?" asked Bors.

"Yes. Rakish even."

"You are a dunderhead," said Bors.

"Here now!" said Hector, stomping over to Bors.

"What's the matter this time?" asked Magdalena, as she and Mel joined the others.

Erec tossed a stone into the river.

"I would say the trouble is that since defeating creatures taller than trees and mightier than dragons, the biggest excitement we've had is the fact that Hector has a tiny new mustache."

"Rakish!" piped Hector. "I thought a change would liven things up a bit."

"We're wandering," said Erec. "We need a proper adventure. Grail hunting is not even close."

They fell into silence.

A fierce wind blew.

And a long, sleek ship sailed silently around the bend in the river. They all watched as it drifted up to the bank and paused, as if docked. No one was onboard. The boat

was beautiful: deep green and black with a fine crimson sail. It was not large, but it could easily hold five people comfortably.

"Ho, ho," murmured Erec.

They all stood and admired the strange ship.

"Well then," said Bors, climbing aboard.

Erec and Hector followed. So did Magdalena.

Mel hesitated.

"Um, should we maybe . . . I mean, perhaps we shouldn't immediately board a crewless boat that we know nothing about? Just a thought."

The others stared blankly at Mel.

"Mel, when a mysterious vessel pulls up, every knight knows exactly what to do," said Erec.

"Instinct," said Magdalena.

"All right then," said Mel.

She adjusted her quiver, swung her bow across her back, and leaped aboard.

The wind picked up and the vessel sailed away.

CHAPTER TWO

AN UNUSUAL OCCURRENCE AT SEA

The mysterious ship sailed on. They glided down the river and eventually out to sea. The ocean was rough and choppy. The conversation onboard was similar.

"All I'm saying is that we could use a *Tyrannosaurus rex* or two to break up the monotony," said Bors.

"That's not an option, Bors. Unless you want to ask Merlin to send us back to the land of terrible lizards," said Erec.

"Gladly," countered Bors.

"Hold on a minute," said Hector. "Let's not get carried away."

"Magdalena," called Erec. "Anything you care to add to this conversation?"

Magdalena sat near the prow, gazing out at the mainland. She merely glanced at the knights before resuming her brooding stare.

"That's what I thought," said Erec.

Mel crossed the deck and stood by the Black Knight.

"Is everything all right, Magdalena?" asked Mel.

Magdalena did not answer.

"I wonder where we are now?" Mel tried.

Magdalena responded without turning. "Scotland."

"Oh. Do you know it well?"

Magdalena fell silent again. Mel waited, but a response was not forthcoming. The Black Knight was not one to be pressed or pushed.

So Mel slipped back to rejoin the others, who were attempting but failing to make progress in their conversation.

"Two of the large spiky-headed ones charging full

steam, plus, say, four of those smaller fast ones with the ankle claws," said Bors. "My first move would require a battle-ax—"

"But this is pointless, Bors," interjected Erec. "There are no terrible lizards in Britain. We need to be practical and we need to focus. A direction. A plan."

"We just jumped onto a boat because it pulled up beside us. That's not really a plan, Sir Erec," said Mel. "We have no idea where we are going."

"At least we are going *somewhere*," observed Hector.

The ship lurched on a large wave. Hector grabbed hold of the side, looking a tad green.

"Although I wish we were doing so on land," he added.

"The boat was a sound move," said Erec. "As leader, I stand behind it."

"As what now?" asked Bors, looking up from a complicated knot he was trying to tie with some spare rope. "Leader? Who?"

"I am," said Erec.

"Since when?"

"Well . . . always. The terrible lizard adventure was due to me," said Erec.

"You instigated it, perhaps," said Hector. "But you didn't lead it per se."

"Even Hector can see that," laughed Bors.

"What do you mean 'even Hector'?" Hector asked loudly.

Thunder boomed. Lightning streaked across the night sky. Dark clouds roiled overhead, and the sea churned and raged. The conversation drifted into silence. The hours dragged on. They were far out to sea now. Eventually Erec sighed.

"Well, so far this magical boat ride has been rather disappointing."

"Patience, fellow knight," said Bors from the stern of the ship.

"*Bors* is advising me to be patient. Everything is topsy-turvy. Perhaps that is the magic. Bors has become sage and reflective."

"Not reflective. Never that," said Bors. "And your

patience will not be required for long, I'm happy to report."

"Why is that?" asked Hector.

"There appears to be something in the water."

Magdalena and Mel looked up. They joined Hector, Erec, and Bors at the rear of the boat.

"I don't see anything," said Erec.

A tremendous wave splashed on the band as a gargantuan creature rose from the depths. It was as tall as the mast, with a face that resembled a perturbed trout mixed with an incensed parrot.

The knights and Mel tumbled across the deck, trying

to regain their balance on the slick surface.

"What *is* it?" yelled Mel.

"I believe it is a kraken, Mel," offered Hector as he was tossed from one end of the deck to the other. "I read about them in a book once. I'm not sure, of course. I would need to check the book again."

"I applaud your optimism, Hector," said Erec, gripping some rope. "But curling up in your library with a good book is unlikely to happen unless we deal with this kraken. NOW."

The kraken lifted the ship and gave it a good shake.

The crew held on to whatever they could grab as the kraken pitched the ship through the air. It landed hard in the water, splintering on impact.

"New plan!" shouted Erec. "Salvage anything that floats!"

The knights began to hack at the ship with swords and axes, pulling up chunks of the ruined deck.

The kraken dove.

"Hurry!" shouted Magdalena.

They all threw the best bits of salvage and barrels overboard and leaped from the ship into the sea just as the kraken surfaced. A massive wave swept the company up and away. They clutched their makeshift rafts and watched as the kraken rolled over the remains of the ship again and again.

The knights and Mel drifted into the darkness and mist, lost at sea.

CHAPTER THREE

WELCOME
TO ORKNEY!

It was a long night. Exhausted, the band clung to whatever salvage they had taken from the ship, holding on for dear life in the cold, relentless sea.

Mel's strength was fading. The pull of the ocean was strong. The waves pounded into her brain. *Come*, they whispered. Her grip loosened, and she slipped off the mast into the current.

At that moment Bors opened his weary eyes.

"Mel!" he called.

He launched himself from his own raft to swim after Mel. Knights, however, are lousy swimmers. It has a lot to do with the chain mail they wear. And the weapons. Nevertheless, Bors flailed his arms in a frenzied approximation of swimming without concern for his own safety.

He went under.

And his belly immediately touched the sandy bottom. The waves rolled over his back, and Bors sat up in surprise. Sitting there, the water only came up to his chest.

He peered into the darkness. Mel was about twenty

feet away. Standing. They had reached land.

They all trudged out of the surf and stumbled up the sandy beach out of the tide before collapsing once again from sheer exhaustion.

Sometime later a boot to the ribs stirred Sir Erec.

"Ow!" he groused.

Erec looked up. Three men were standing over the knights. It was morning, but a gray, bleak sort of morning.

Erec sat up slowly. He squinted at the tallest of the men.

"Agravaine?"

He turned to the second man.

"Gareth?"

Erec looked up at the brute who had kicked him. He was the roughest looking of the bunch.

"I don't know you."

The brute kicked him again.

"*Stop* it! I can tell from your manners that you're related. Don't tell me. We're in Orkney."

Agravaine took a step closer.

"The Orkney Isles. A place of wild beauty and noble history. A land of—"

"Save it for the tourists, Agravaine," grumbled Bors. "We need a ship to take us back to civilization."

The brutish one took a menacing stomp toward Bors. Agravaine held up a hand.

"No, Gorp. Perhaps you do not know. This *band* is the very same that battled the so-called terrible lizards. They are honored guests."

"Guests of whom?" asked Magdalena.

Agravaine faced her with a smile.

"Why, Queen Morgause, of course. Come, Black Knight. She is expecting you."

The knights and Mel got to their feet and followed the Orkneys up a path from the shore. No one spoke, but all were alert to their surroundings, and more importantly, to their company.

A word about the Orkneys. The Orkney Isles are located north of Scotland. They are wild, untamed islands with a long history of magic and legendary heroes. King Lot ruled them with Queen Morgause until his rebellion was put to an end by a young King Arthur. Arthur's father also had run-ins with the Orkney Clan, with mostly bad results. So although Gawain, Agravaine, and Gareth were all Knights of the Round Table, plenty of "bad blood" and old grudges were still in the mix. Sir Gawain was an exemplary knight, the others less so.

They entered a village that sat below the dark keep of a castle. The homes were small and modest, dried mud or stone structures with wood doors, shuttered windows, and thatched roofs. As the company passed, a few villagers peered out of windows or doorways. None waved. Not one smiled. It was strangely quiet.

"Hello, villagers!" said Hector pleasantly.

Bors eyed a couple of the men. They stared back with hardened faces. The women held their children close.

"They don't seem pleased to see us," whispered Mel.

"Oh, you know how it is in places like Orkney," said Erec. "'Remote' doesn't even begin to describe it. They're not used to visitors. Especially Knights of the Round Table."

"Hail, Sir Gawain!" one of the village women called out.

"No, I am Sir Erec. Gawain is back in Camelot," called Erec to blank stares. "Cam-e-lot."

"Our brother Gawain is much loved, Sir Erec," said Agravaine. "Even when he is forced to be in England, his heart remains here in Orkney."

"Oh, right," said Erec. "Of course."

They continued on the muddy road toward the castle. It was foreboding but simple, no flourishes like spires or even banners.

The castle was the same dark gray of the Orkney sky. Mysterious, cold, and unwelcoming.

"Home," grunted Gorp.

A long rectangular table had been set in a drafty hall lit by a few torches and a hearth fire. A smaller table sat in the corner. A very somber boy sat at that one. He was a few years younger than Mel, well dressed in black velvet with eyes that matched his garment. He was pasty pale and rather thin. The boy stood as they approached.

Agravaine gestured to Mel.

"You. You are to sit with our youngest brother, Mordred."

"Mel is one of us," said Magdalena.

"Mother's request," answered Agravaine. "She thinks Mordred and . . . *Mel* . . . will amuse each other."

Mel eyed Mordred. Mordred's lips spread awkwardly in an attempt at a smile. Mel glanced at Magdalena, who nodded. Mel trudged over to the small table.

"Pleased to meet you," said Mordred, pulling out a chair. "I am Mordred. I am the special one."

"Oh?" said Mel. "That's nice for you. Why are you special?"

"Mother says so," he said simply. "Isn't that right, Brother Agravaine?"

Agravaine eyed his youngest brother.

"Yes," said Agravaine. "For some reason."

A feast was laid out for the company. But it was not festive. The knights made stabs at conversation, but the Orkney Boys spoke only sparingly. There was neither music nor jester. The hours crawled.

"So," said Hector, finally, "will we be meeting Morgause this evening?"

Gorp and Gareth paused mid-chew.

"*Queen* Morgause," said Gareth. "She is still queen to all on this isle, regardless of current circumstances."

"But she does not dine with you?" asked Bors. "Arthur always eats with the knights."

"Mother is not Arthur," said Gareth.

"Obviously," said Bors.

"If she summons us, we will go," said Agravaine. "*If.*"

Mel ate in silence, occasionally glancing at Mordred, who for the most part simply stared back at Mel.

"What is it?" demanded Mel.

Mordred tipped his head.

"Say something," said Mel.

"You are unusual."

"Maybe I'm special, like you."

"No, not special. *Unusual.*"

Mel rolled her eyes and sipped her drink.

"You are a peasant," said Mordred. "Yet you do not

dress like a squire."

"I am not a squire. I am an archer."

"You are a child."

Mel set her cup down.

"I have seen things you cannot imagine. I may be young, but I am an adventurer, I assure you."

Mordred leaned in, squinting.

"Very interesting," he whispered.

"Most of the time," said Mel, looking longingly across the room.

Things were heating up at the big table.

"He didn't mean there was something *wrong* with the table," offered Erec. "Bors just pointed out that it is rectangular in shape."

"Which is factually correct," added Hector.

"And therefore it is inferior to a round table," said Bors.

Erec put his hand to his head.

"Inferior? How dare thee!" barked Gareth.

"I do dare," said Bors.

Gorp rose.

Bors rose.

"Enough!" shouted Agravaine.

"It took longer than I would have wagered to get to this point, Sir Agravaine," said Erec. "Perhaps, if the queen is tired, we could go to our lodging and—"

A great gong sounded through the chamber. The Orkneys turned in unison to an enormous black door. They looked uncertain and a bit uneasy.

"The queen will see you now," said Agravaine quietly.

CHAPTER FOUR

BAD PLAYDATE

As the group marched down the hallway, Mordred grasped Mel's arm with his bony little fingers.

"You are to come with me!"

"No," said Mel, removing the fingers. "I am to stay with my companions."

"That's just it," hissed Mordred. "Mother says that you are to be *my* companion!"

"But . . ."

"You'd better go, Mel," said Erec. "We do not wish to

offend Queen Morgause. We will find you later."

Mel fumed but followed Mordred down a different hall.

Mordred led Mel into a large chamber.

"This is my nursery," Mordred said proudly. "*My* room."

Mel looked around the torchlit chamber.

"Are those . . . skulls?" she asked.

"The mist will come soon!" said Mordred with excitement.

Mel was still eyeing the skulls that decorated the playroom. There were also several stuffed animal specimens, books, and crystals of all sizes.

"There is always mist in Scotland," said Mel.

"Not like this," he chuckled. "Have you ever seen a monster? A real live monster?"

"Yes," said Mel.

"You have seen animals of great size, Melancholy." He laughed. "But you have not seen a monster."

"What is going on?" demanded Mel.

"Mother's wonderful plan is beginning. It is the reason she brought those knights to Orkney. Monsters, Mel. Real monsters."

Mel was at the door.

"It's locked. Open it, Mordred."

"You don't want to go out there."

"Open it!"

"Stay here with me. We can listen to the screams together."

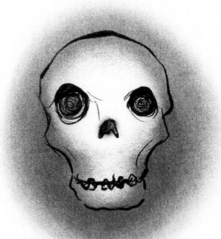

CHAPTER FIVE

WELCOME TO THE NIGHTMARE!

The throne room of Castle Lot was not large, but the high ceilings and few torches made it imposing. Stone stairs led up to a dais in the far corner of the room to the throne.

"Approach," said Morgause quietly. The knights knelt at the foot of the stairs.

"So. Arthur's bravest knights."

"Queen Morgause, we bring greetings and respect. We are in need of a ship so that we might return to

England," said Erec, bowing his head.

"Return to England," repeated the queen.

"Yes," said Erec. "Please."

Morgause stared intensely at Magdalena. The Black Knight held her gaze.

"We have not properly met," said Morgause.

"I am Sir Bors. You must have heard of—"

"SILENCE!" Morgause's voice rose and stung like a wasp. "I was not speaking to you, knight."

"I am Magdalena, the Black Knight, Your Highness," said Magdalena calmly.

"The *Black Knight* of . . . Camelot."

"Yes."

A pause.

"Ah, Your Majesty? About that boat?" began Erec.

"I have already provided you with a ship, good knight."

"Um . . ."

"The enchanted boat, Sir Erec," explained Magdalena. "Queen Morgause sent it."

"Good gracious. How could she?" said Hector. "One

would need to know sorcery to . . ." He trailed off, looking up at Morgause. "Ohhhh."

Morgause smiled coolly, then stood and crossed the dais to a window.

"I have summoned you, the knights who battled the terrible lizards, the bravest knights of the Round Table. I have a task for you," continued Morgause. "The creatures of nightmare are loose in the mist and darkness. They are coming. For you."

"Coming for us?" scoffed Bors. "Fine!"

"You said 'in the mist,'" said Hector. "What if we just stay inside? Until the mist clears?"

Morgause gazed out the window. The mist blew from the ocean, obscuring the full moon.

"The mist seems to be heading for the village. How unfortunate," she said.

"But . . . those are your own subjects," said Erec.

Morgause returned to her throne.

"I shall have new subjects very soon. More than you can count," said Morgause.

The flames in the great hall flickered. Silence. The Orkney Boys opened the chamber doors. A scream, faint but clear, sounded from the village below. The knights rushed out without another word.

Morgause smiled, closed her eyes, and listened.

CHAPTER SIX

THICK AS SOUP
AND TWICE AS DEADLY

Erec, Bors, Hector, and Magdalena stormed out of the castle and hurried down the road toward the village. The mist had engulfed the houses. Screams, yells, gasps, and various breaking noises filled the thick air.

They approached the village gate, and the strange mist immediately swallowed them. It was difficult to see anything. Cries for help seemed to come from every direction.

"Split up," said Erec.

Each knight darted in a different direction, swords at the ready.

Bors stumbled on a rock.

"Blast it," he grunted, and kicked the stone.

Silence.

Then the stone was kicked back at Bors.

Bors peered into the impenetrable mist.

"I have neither time nor patience for games. Show yourself now!"

The unmistakable sound of a sword being drawn came from somewhere close.

Bors stood ready. A shape formed in the mist: large, bulky. Two legs. The shadow approached.

"Ah, good. A warrior of some kind. Knight?"

No answer.

"Of course not. Berserker, I wager. One of those fellows who put paint on their faces and hollers a lot? I knew the talk of 'monsters' was an exaggeration."

The figure stepped out of the gloom. It wore armor. It held a sword and an ax. But this was no human. It was huge

and incredibly ugly, with a thick jaw and massive sharp teeth. Horns poked through its helmet. It smelled horrible.

"Oh . . . ," said Bors.

The hideous warrior roared.

"Whatever," said Bors as he raised his sword for battle.

Mel banged on the heavy door of the playroom.

Mordred stood across the room near the window, his thin, pale face lit by candles.

"Mother wants only Arthur's knights to fight the monsters, you see. You are not a knight. You may stay here with Mordred. Lucky, lucky girl."

"Stop talking and give me the key, Mordred."

"I wonder what sort of monsters will come out of the mist. I do wish I could see for myself."

"I can arrange that. The *key*, Mordred."

"Imagine the wonderful horror—"

THWISH! THWUNK!

Mel's arrow pinned Mordred's sleeve to the oak wardrobe behind him.

And she had another arrow poised to fly.

"The key, Mordred," said Mel.

"Third drawer on the left," whimpered Mordred.

Sir Erec felt his way along a stone wall. He knew he was close to the small huts. He hoped the villagers were locked in safely.

A low growl came from behind the wall. Erec stopped.

Slowly, slowly, he looked over the top of the wall.

A small, furry creature with large eyes and large feet crouched in the heather. It bared its tiny sharp teeth but dug into the heather a bit more.

Then something chattered behind Erec. He turned as the chattering gained in intensity, a cacophony of guttural noises and an unrecognizable language.

Erec wasn't sure where to look.

"Pipe down!" he bellowed.

The noise ceased. Erec paused, pleased.

"Now I want you all to gather where I can see you. I am Sir Erec of the—"

What happened next was breathtaking in its speed. Hundreds of small, big-eyed, biting creatures swarmed Erec, pulling his clothes, nibbling his ears, and dragging him backward until he tumbled over the wall.

"Stop it!"

Erec thrashed, tossing several beasties against the wall. But more came.

More always came.

✿ ✿ ✿

Mel locked Mordred in his chamber and hurried down the hallway, careful not to make a sound. She tried to retrace her steps, but every hall looked similar in the dark. She found herself in a passage that looked out over the feasting hall. Agravaine, Gareth, and Gorp sat, huddled by the fire. Mel crept to the edge of the parapet, hidden behind a curtain. She listened.

"How many hours, do you reckon?" asked Gareth.

"No idea," said Agravaine. "They are knights, after all. And they have fought against monstrous creatures before."

"You sound like you admire them," spat Gareth.

"I do not underestimate them. Believe me, brother. I am confident in Mother's plan. The Band of the Terrible Lizards will not last long."

"When can we see?" asked Gorp. "But Gorp does not want to see the monsters," he added quickly.

"Of course not, Gorp," said Agravaine. "We shall wait until morning. Mother says when the dawn breaks, the mist and monsters will retreat until the next nightfall."

"We will go to the village and gather the remains of King Arthur's bravest knights," began Gareth.

"And sail with the bodies to Camelot as a message from the great and terrible Queen Morgause," said Agravaine.

He tossed another log onto the blazing fire. It sparked and spat.

Hector was unsettled. He was never one for night escapades to begin with. Add on this supernatural mist and the thought of lurking monsters and well . . . the conditions were less than ideal.

Still, villagers needed protection, and he was a brave knight. He wandered off the road, stepping gingerly on the moor. For a brief moment, the clouds cleared and a full moon shone down on him. He was not alone.

A small, skinny villager stood there.

"Oh, hello," said Hector. "Don't be frightened. I am Sir Hector. I shall escort you back to the village."

The man stared at Hector, wide-eyed and silent. He trembled violently.

"Cold, eh?" asked Hector. "It does get a bit nippy on these islands. You should know that. Where is your cloak?"

A clank of swords and grunts sounded from somewhere in the mist. Hector peered around but could not see the source of the commotion.

"Well, we best be getting along. Come on."

Without looking back, Hector reached out and took the fellow by the arm.

"Oh. You *do* have a coat. This fur should keep you toasty."

Hector turned to the man. He was not wearing a fur coat.

The man's tunic was, in fact, ripping open, his body contorting, fur sprouting all over him. His nose had grown long like a snout, his eyes turned golden, his teeth sharpened into fangs.

"I say . . . ," began Hector, backing up, sword raised.

The man howled in the most bloodcurdling manner imaginable.

"Golly," Hector whispered.

Mel strained to hear the conversation below. She leaned out from behind the curtain slightly.

"Arthur and all of his subjects will know that monsters are in their midst, monsters that no knight can slay. Fear will spread like a plague. Arthur will lose the confidence of his court, his people, the world," continued Agravaine.

Gorp giggled. "And Mother—"

"Yes," interrupted Gareth. "Mother will arrive in

England. Mother will suppress the monsters. And Mother—Queen Morgause, rightful ruler—will avenge our father and kill our dear uncle Arthur."

Mel gasped.

Agravaine looked up.

The Black Knight was utterly alone in the mist. She stood still as a stone cairn. Her eyes were closed. She was listening.

The voices were faint at first, like a breeze rustling

leaves. But they were becoming clearer. There were many voices—men, women, children—all speaking at once.

They were saying terrible things.

Magdalena did not shut out the voices. She listened to each one.

She breathed.

The voices became more shrill. They surrounded her. They pelted her with ideas, with opinions, with observations.

About her.

Mel slid down and scuttled across the stone floor.

"Gorp, see what that was," said Agravaine.

Both sides of the hallway ended in stairs that led down to the dining chamber. There was no way out.

Gorp thumped up one of the stairs.

A single window was cut into the thick wall. Mel leaped to the edge of the window and looked out. A drop of a hundred feet lay below her. But to the right and perhaps twenty feet over was the roof of a small tower.

She closed her eyes and took a breath. And then she

slipped out the window, digging her fingers into small crevices in the wall. She inched away. The wind whipped, cold and cruel.

She managed to climb several feet away from the window before she had to pause.

As if on cue, Gorp stuck his head out of the window. He looked down but of course saw nothing. His head disappeared back into the window.

Mel let out a relieved breath. Slowly, carefully, she continued her creep along the craggy castle wall.

She did not look down. She did not think of the height. She cleared her mind like a good archer and concentrated only on each small, incremental move.

She tried not to listen to the screams that came from the village. She tried not to think of the mist and the monsters and the fate of her companions.

She tried.

A bead of sweat trickled down Magdalena's brow. She clenched her fists, then released them. The voices raged.

Her eyes opened.

"Enough," she said.

The voices ceased.

Silence.

Then a large, ugly monster hurtled out of the mist and landed in front of her with a thud.

The monster growled, struggled to its feet, and swung its ax.

"I *said*," bellowed Bors, bursting out of the mist, sword raised, "STAY. DOWN."

He buried his sword in the monster a second before its ax reached the Black Knight.

Bors finally noticed Magdalena.

"Oh, hello. I got one. A monster. Bit of a bother, but not too bad. How about you? Any monsters?"

"No," said Magdalena. "No monsters."

The mist was thinning as the sun began to rise.

Erec and Hector stumbled into view. Erec's tunic was shredded. Hector was physically fine but nervously looking behind him.

"All in one piece? Excellent," said Erec. "Let's check on the villagers. I don't think we've seen the end of this."

CHAPTER SEVEN

KNIGHTS VS. VILLAGERS

After the long night of scaling the castle wall, Mel shivered in the morning chill. She was perched on the roof of the small tower, blowing gently on her raw fingertips and considering her options. She was still a good thirty feet above the ground.

"Hoy!" called a voice from below.

Mel scrambled to the edge. Sir Hector sat in a horse-drawn cart that was loaded with straw.

"Or rather . . . hay!" he chuckled. "I noticed your plight

from the road and managed to . . . er . . . borrow this cart."

Mel smiled and jumped, landing softly in the piled hay. Hector jerked the reins, and the horse ambled onward.

Mel joined Hector on the seat of the cart.

"We knew you could take care of yourself," said Hector, "but I didn't much like the idea of you up here at the castle with these Orkney royals."

He lowered his voice to a whisper. "They're not terribly nice."

Mel smiled and gave Hector a little hug.

"You have a good heart, Sir Hector."

Hector pish-poshed but smiled.

"We need our archer. Things got a little hairy last night. Quite literally, in some cases," he added.

"I heard the screams," said Mel. "And I also heard something else, something I need to tell all of you."

Hector snapped the reins, and the cart sped down the road to the village.

✿ ✿ ✿

"Please, if you would all just quiet down," said Sir Erec.

Erec, Bors, and Magdalena stood by a stone wall, addressing the villagers who had gathered in the small square.

"Now, is everyone present and accounted for?" asked Erec.

Murmurs and a few quizzical looks came in answer.

"Did anyone get eaten or mauled to death last night? No? Splendid! You're welcome."

Silence from the crowd.

"Ingrates," muttered Bors.

"Unfortunately, I do not believe we are out of the woods yet . . . so to speak . . . I mean . . . I know you don't actually *have* woods on the island, but you know what woods *are*. Don't you?"

A very tall, red-haired woman at the front of the crowd threw a handful of mud at Erec.

"Hey!" said Erec.

"We know what woods are. And monsters. And so-called Knights of the Round Table. What are you going to

do about all this?" said the woman.

"You are right to be angry," said Magdalena. "We know the people of the Orkneys are strong and brave. We are counting on it. Still, some of you might be frightened."

Bors cut in.

"But you are in luck! We're here!" He spread his arms wide. He waited for some sort of acknowledgment or possibly applause. None came.

"What Sir Bors means," said Erec quickly, "is that we will protect you. We have experience with . . . unusual creatures."

"That's just it," said the red-haired woman. "We don't need your protection. We have the Sons of Orkney and our beloved Queen Morgause."

"But they are the ones who brought the monsters!"

All turned to see Mel walking up with Hector.

"I heard them. Sir Agravaine, Sir Gareth, and . . . the other one. They were plotting."

"Lies!" shouted several villagers.

"No," said Mel firmly. "Queen Morgause summoned

the monsters to kill us as a message to King Arthur. If any of you dies as well, so be it. None of her sons will protect you."

Another silence fell over the crowd.

And then a lone clapping came from the road. Agravaine approached with Gareth and Gorp behind him.

"What a fine tale!" said Agravaine. "Sir Erec, I did not know that your child sidekick was a storyteller. Does she also juggle?"

"She can send an arrow between your eyes at a hundred paces," said Bors.

Mel held her tongue. Agravaine's insult had angered her, but at that moment she was more shocked by the compliment from Bors. She stole a glance at him. He did not look at her.

"Tut, tut," said Agravaine. "We're all friends here."

Agravaine leaped up to the wall.

"Villagers!" he called. "These strangers are not telling you the truth. We did not have monsters in Orkney before they arrived. That is a fact."

"True!" added Gareth.

"Arrgh!" chipped in Gorp.

"I am not saying that these knights are the cause; it's just an observation. I am sure they will fight bravely for you, as shall we," continued Agravaine. "Now, return to your daily lives. This will all end very soon."

The villagers seemed relieved. They clapped and dispersed happily. The red-haired woman held back for a moment. She looked at Agravaine, then at Erec.

Erec held her gaze but said nothing.

She walked off with the others.

The knights and Mel stared at the Orkney Boys. The Orkneys stared back.

"Well," began Erec.

"Well," answered Agravaine.

"We had an interesting night. Nothing we couldn't handle, obviously," said Erec.

"You'll not fare so well tonight!" growled Gareth.

"Would you care to wager on that?" asked Hector coolly.

"Grrr," said Gorp.

"Grrrrr," retorted Bors.

"Is this posturing going to go on all day, or is there some point to our talking?" said Magdalena.

"We've nothing to hear from you, traitor," sneered Gareth.

Magdalena's leg swiped out so fast no one was sure exactly what happened. But Gareth was flat on his back in the road with Magdalena standing over him.

"Stay down," she said quietly.

Gareth said nothing but shot a look at Agravaine.

"Forgive my brother, Black Knight. He lacks the social manners required of a knight of Camelot. That's why he spends so much time here in Orkney," said Agravaine.

He strolled over to stand in front of Magdalena.

"Gareth," Agravaine continued pointedly, "knows his true home."

Magdalena glared at Agravaine but remained silent.

Agravaine walked back to Erec.

"Your jester—"

"Archer!" said Mel.

"Sorry. *Archer* is correct, of course. But the villagers needn't know that," said Agravaine.

"You, Agravaine, like your brother Sir Gawain, swore allegiance to Arthur."

Agravaine leaned close to Erec.

"Unlike my *brother* Gawain, my allegiance is to Mother, first and always. If you are wise, you will bow down to Queen Morgause."

"I thought the plan was to kill us. Why bow down just to get killed?" said Bors. "Ha! Gotcha there, Aggie."

Gorp stood up to his full height and took a menacing step toward Bors.

"Watch it, Lesser Orkney," said Bors.

"GORP!"

"I'll gorp you right into the sea."

"Brothers! We are wasting our time. Let us leave them to enjoy their last day on Earth."

"See you tomorrow, then," said Erec with a smile.

The Orkney Boys skulked back to the castle. When they were out of earshot, Agravaine addressed his brothers.

"I've no more patience. I shall sail today for England to spread word of their defeat. If they survive the night . . . kill them."

CHAPTER EIGHT

OF BLOODSUCKING FIENDS

All through the day, the villagers gathered supplies, repaired broken doors and shutters, and sharpened pitchforks. Livestock were secured in stables. Cats were herded.

Mel practiced her archery, sending arrow after arrow into a post by the stables.

Thwick!

Thwack!

Thwunk!

She made a perfect vertical line of arrows.

"The last one is a bit high."

It was Bors, who had been watching Mel, unbeknownst to her.

"True, Sir Bors. That is why I am practicing."

Mel selected an arrow. She let it fly and it hit the mark perfectly.

"Not bad," said Bors.

Mel walked to the post and began to remove the arrows.

"You have learned well, I'll admit," said Bors.

"Magdalena is a good teacher," said Mel, without looking back. "I've learned more from her than anyone has ever taught me."

"Well, I do take *some* credit," said Bors, examining his fingernails.

Mel paused and turned back.

"You, Sir Bors? How do you reckon that?"

"You *were* my squire, after all—"

"I carried your weapons and shined your armor."

"And deceived me into thinking you were a lad."

"Yes," said Mel. "That, too."

"*Which* led me to sack you. You then had the free time to learn about archery and fighting and all sorts of new skills."

"Yes, but—"

"So, you see, you ought to thank me," said Bors. "But no need, Mel. No need. Just as long as you and everyone else knows."

Mel smiled, despite herself.

"Yes, Sir Bors. Everyone knows all about you."

"Good," said Bors. "Carry on."

Bors strode off whistling a little tune. Mel shook her head and then in a flash, swiveled and shot an arrow into the post. Direct hit.

Sir Erec made the rounds inspecting the doors and gates of various huts. It was thankless work, quite literally. No one said a single word to him, unless sighs and *hmffs!* count.

The tall red-haired woman leaned against her open door, watching Erec approach.

"Do you have a bolt for that door?" asked Erec.

She narrowed her eyes at him, then walked into her home.

Erec inspected the door.

"Pretty sturdy, I guess."

The woman banged a few pots.

Erec wandered in.

"So. Just you in this charming hovel, then?" Erec asked, looking around the room.

She busied herself in the corner and did not answer.

"No . . . uh . . . husband?"

More pots were banged.

Erec inspected a shelf that was decorated with seashells and small clay figurines.

"Or a boyfriend?"

He lifted one of the figures gently. It was in an action pose.

"Wait. Is this Agravaine?"

The woman swung around.

"Put that down!"

"It is, isn't it? They're all little Agravaines," Erec said, examining the clay figures.

"What are you doing here? Get out!"

"I'm just trying to, you know, make sure everything is secure—"

"Get. Out!"

"And I saw these little statues and . . . just making conversation."

She lifted an iron pan.

"Out. Now."

"Right."

Erec went to the door and paused. "I am sorry to bother you, um . . ."

"Greer," said the woman.

"Greer? That's . . . that's a pretty name."

Greer glared.

"Okay. Bolt the door tonight and all that, Greer."

Erec ducked out quickly.

Magdalena perched on the edge of a cliff, staring at the crashing surf. She sat motionless, save for her red hair whipping violently in the wind.

"Magdalena?" Mel had to raise her voice to be heard.

Without turning around Magdalena gestured for Mel to approach.

Mel climbed onto a rock by her side. She gazed at the ocean, the rocks, the pounding and relentless waves. It was bleak and dangerous, but beautiful.

"Do you like it here? In Orkney," asked Mel. "Aside from the monsters, of course?"

"You might as well ask if I like my bones or muscle," said Magdalena.

"You've been here before?" asked Mel.

After a few moments of silence, Mel rose. "I'll leave you in peace."

"I was born in Scotland," Magdalena said. "At least that's what I've been told. I don't remember the land . . . and yet I recognize every stone. Odd, isn't it?"

Mel listened silently.

"My mother was from these isles. But she came to England with my father and never returned. She didn't speak of it. And then she died."

Mel took a step closer.

"Do you think—"

"Always have one arrow at the ready tonight. Shoot and, as you release, reach for your next arrow in one motion. Do not hesitate," interrupted Magdalena.

The Black Knight stood and turned her back to the sea.

"We should be getting ready."

She passed Mel and started down the path toward the village. Mel watched her for a moment before following.

It was dusk. The villagers were shut indoors. All was quiet.

The knights and Mel were in the square.

"I hate waiting," said Bors.

"You could take this moment to prepare mentally. Clear your mind for the battle to come," said Hector brightly. "I find it useful to—"

"Hector, there is nothing you could ever say that I would consider useful," said Bors.

"I was only suggesting," Hector sniffed.

"Ugh! Come, monsters, so I can stop listening to Hector's prattling!"

"You started it," muttered Hector.

"We should all concentrate, I think," said Erec. "We have no idea what is coming."

"We only know when," said Magdalena, nodding to the distance.

A mist was creeping low across the ground, blowing in from the coast and seeping up from the crags in the earth. It slithered toward the village like a million snakes, slow at first, then building, growing thicker and faster.

Mel breathed in and out slowly. She took an arrow from her quiver.

"Tight perimeter, fellows," said Erec. "Fight together. Stay close to the village. Slay anything that comes out of that mist."

The knights took their positions. Mel found a spot near Magdalena.

Bors whistled a low tune as he tossed his ax casually into the air, catching it by the handle and tossing it up again. Up and down. Up and down.

The mist crawled closer and closer.

Bors stopped whistling and caught his ax.

All was silent and still.

And then it began.

✿ ✿ ✿

Magdalena and the Rabid Rapscallion

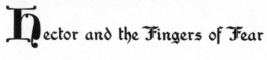
Hector and the Fingers of Fear

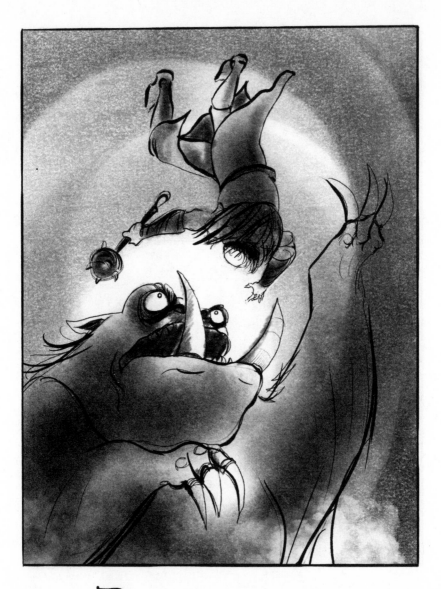

Bors and the Boarish Beast

Erec and the Eel of Misery

Mel and the Oozing 'Orror

The night was nearly over, and the monsters, sensing the dawn, had begun to retreat.

Erec chased a nasty-looking goblin through the village, finally cornering it by a wall and slaying it.

A candle burned in one of the homes nearby. The door was wide open.

"Greer," breathed Erec.

He approached warily. There was not a sound from inside. Sword ready, Erec slipped in. He rounded the corner that led to Greer's bedchamber.

Greer was lying in bed, asleep. And a rail-thin, pale figure with a bald high-domed head, pointed ears, and wide eyes was leaning over her. Its lips parted, exposing two long, sharp fangs.

With a ratlike squeak, the fiend bit Greer on the neck.

"Oi!" shouted Erec.

Strangely Greer did not wake, but the creature looked up, a trail of blood dribbling down its chin.

Erec lunged, but the monster held up one hand, its long, spidery fingers outstretched. An invisible force threw Erec back. He hit the wall and collapsed to the floor.

Erec rose, but the creature smiled and raised its hand once more, pinning Erec against the wall. It raised its hand higher and Erec lifted off the ground.

The fiend hissed at him, waving its hand to the left and dragging Erec in the same direction. Erec was powerless.

He scraped along the wall until he reached a mirror that hung there. The creature halted. It tilted its head.

Erec followed its gaze to the mirror. There was no reflection, which seemed to baffle the creature as much as it did Erec.

Taking advantage of the distraction, Erec pushed off the wall with all his might and broke the spell, landing squarely on the monster.

It squealed as they scuffled. Erec got a few good punches in. He grabbed the creature by the collar and—

Poof!

The fiend was gone. A bat fluttered in its place for a moment before darting out the door.

Greer moaned softly as she woke. When she saw Erec, she sat up with a start.

"What are you doing here?!"

"There was a . . . It—it was biting your neck!" stammered Erec.

Greer reached up to feel the two little bite marks on her neck. She drew her hand away and stared at the blood on her fingertips.

"What—" she began.

POOF

The bat zipped back into the room, returned to its original shape, and took a bite of Erec's neck.

"AH! Get off me!"

Erec shoved it. He took a swing and *poof* the fiend was a bat. Then *poof* back to fiend for another nibble of Erec. Erec punched. *Poof*. Bat.

The bat fluttered behind Erec and changed once again.

BAM!

Greer whacked the monster on the head with her iron pan, sending it tumbling out the door.

Erec was after it in an instant. The fiend scrambled to its feet, backing away.

The mist was thinning. A single beam from the rising sun broke through and struck the fiend on the shoulder.

"EEEP!" it cried, hopping out of the beam, shoulder smoldering.

Erec and the creature stood still for a moment, contemplating this new development.

Erec stepped forward and nudged the fiend into the beam of light again.

"ERP!" it cried, and jumped out.

Erec prodded it back in.

The mist cleared, the sunbeam widened, and . . .

WHOOSH!

The fiend disintegrated into a small pile of dust.

"Hmm," said Erec, kicking the dust with idle curiosity.

The mist dissipated completely, and the early morning sun shone a golden orange.

Erec turned back to Greer, who stood speechless in the doorway, holding her neck.

Erec nodded.

"Ma'am."

And he strode off to find the others.

He found them all in the stables, collapsed with exhaustion.

Erec fell face-first into a pile of hay.

"I hate this place," he said.

CHAPTER NINE

A STRANGE LITTLE LAD

Mordred set a small cauldron on the fire he had built in the center of a ring of tall stones, each with carvings in an ancient language.

He stirred his potion, adding bits of herbs and less-innocent ingredients from a small pouch.

The liquid grew thick, purplish in color, and slightly luminescent.

He felt very proud of himself.

Mel walked past the ring of stones, stifling a yawn.

"Hello, Mel!" said Mordred, standing. "What a pleasant surprise."

Mel sighed and walked over.

"You have not been eaten by a monster yet?" asked Mordred.

"Apparently not," said Mel.

"Can you describe one to me? A monster? I am oh, so curious."

Mel narrowed her eyes. "Why don't you stick around tonight and see for yourself?"

"Mother would not like that."

"Of course not," said Mel. She wandered over to a standing stone, tracing the runes with her finger.

"Those are monuments to the Ancient Ones. My ancestors. Orkney is a source of great magic and power."

"But what do they do?" asked Mel. "This ring of stones here?"

Mordred paused.

"I do not know exactly."

"Hmm," said Mel.

"One can channel the magic if one knows how. Would you care to look into my cauldron?"

"No."

"But . . . it is . . . quite beautiful."

"No, thank you."

"It smells like flowers."

"Is that so? I must be off, Mordred."

Mel returned to the road.

Mordred stood, incensed.

"Look into my cauldron!"

"Get bent."

Mordred lowered his voice.

"You will regret how you spoke to me, peasant. I am destined for greatness, for legend. They will one day sing heroic songs that proclaim my name."

"Doubtful with a name like that," said Mel. "Mordred. More dread. Not very heroic."

Mordred looked suddenly crestfallen.

"Mother calls me her little Dreadful."

"You are a weird child, Mordred," said Mel as she walked on down the lane.

Mordred stewed. He stared at his cauldron. All that work. All those preparations. Mother would have been so impressed with her little Dreadful.

"Oh, hello there!" Sir Hector ambled up to the ring of stones. "Mordred, isn't it? I was just doing a bit of sightseeing before tonight's nightmarish activities."

Mordred perked up.

"Can you describe a monster for me?"

"Oh. Well . . . none of them are very pleasant."

"Anything would do. Please, sir knight."

Hector considered.

"The first night I met a chap who looked human but then wasn't so much."

"Go on!"

"He sprouted fur and fangs and went all *arrgh* on me. It was as if he were a wolf."

"Were a wolf?"

"Were a wolf."

"Were a wolf," said Mordred with relish. "How did you vanquish it? Did you run it through with your sword?"

"I tried," said Hector, "but I missed, actually. Then while swinging around for another go, I bonked it rather hard on the head with the hilt. It went down, and that was that."

"Fascinating!" said Mordred. "Was there silver in the hilt?"

"A bit," said Hector.

"Extraordinary."

"Fairly common, actually," said Hector.

Mordred was lost in his thoughts for a moment.

Hector wandered up to the cauldron.

"What do you have here?" he asked.

Mordred focused on Hector. A thin, reptilian smile unfurled across his pale face.

"Have a look."

Hector leaned over the cauldron. A purple mist spilled out and engulfed him. There was no time to call for help.

CHAPTER TEN

BI-CLOPS!

"Where's Hector?" asked Erec, as the knights and Mel gathered in the square before sundown.

"Probably doing something daft like sightseeing," said Bors.

Hours later . . .

"Where's Hector?!"

The night's onslaught had been worse than the

previous nights; fiercer, with more monsters than ever. First came a small horde of sword-wielding skeletons. Those were joined by winged harpies screeching and swooping down with fiendish claws. The knights' swords and Mel's arrows beat them back, but with great effort.

Mel faced off with a giant wooden man, which gave her particular trouble since each arrow seemed to only tickle it. Bors and his ax finished that job.

More came: strange creatures like bears with rhino heads, skulls that ran on little hands, and some that defy description. The night raged on and the heroes fought with all their might, but Hector's absence was sorely felt.

"Hector! We need you! Now!"

The Black Knight and Mel battled a monster with deadly tentacles that hid itself deep in the mist, striking with the speed of a viper.

Bors and Erec were ambushed by a giant brute that tossed them against the wall of a hut before they could even get a look at it.

Winded, they slowly rallied their strength.

The sound of enormous feet crunched toward them.

They froze, eyes on the dark mist. A monster emerged from the gloom. It was huge, terrifying, fierce, and—

"Wait," said Erec. "Is that a wee mustache?"

The monster before them had an ugly, brutish face with a single eye in the forehead. It had a *second* head next to the first, also with a single eye in the forehead. This face, while still quite ugly, sported a small mustache that one might consider dashing or perhaps even rakish.

"Hector?" asked Erec.

The two-headed cyclops paused. The mustached head changed its angry expression to one of puzzlement. The other head remained rather monstrous and angry. The creature rapped the mustached head with its own hand.

The mustached head turned to the other head and they began to argue in a strange tongue.

Mel and Magdalena joined the group and stood staring at the bi-clops.

"What in blazes is going on?" asked Bors.

"I think . . . I think that's Hector. On the left," said Erec.

Mel gasped.

The mustached head looked back to the group, its eye wide as if trying to communicate. The angry head bared its teeth at the other head and roared. Then the two-headed cyclops ran off into the mist.

CHAPTER ELEVEN

AND THEN THERE WERE FOUR

The following day, the heroes tried to focus on the now-daily tasks.

IN THE LOCH?

YES! I CLEARLY SAW A HEAD, LONG NECK, BUMPY BACK, AND TAIL.

I DON'T SEE ANYTHING NOW, BUT WE'LL LOOK INTO IT.

CAN'T HAVE A MONSTER LIVING IN YOUR LOCH, CAN WE?

At night, the monsters returned with renewed fury. There were new horrors, but the knights were interested in only one particular monster now.

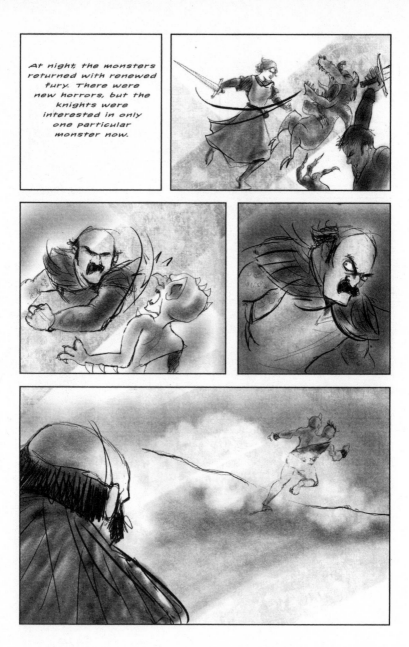

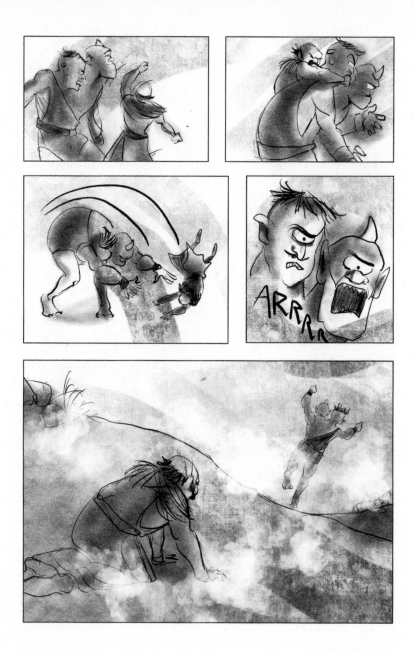

Bors slowly rose to his feet, his eyes set on the direction the bi-clops took. He scowled and stomped after it.

"What are you doing, Bors?" called Erec.

Bors turned but did not stop.

"Doing my job. Killing monsters." He vanished into the darkness.

Two gorilla-sized ogres launched an attack, knocking over Erec and Magdalena. They were up again in a flash, swords swinging.

Mel paused for moment, then tore off into the mist after Bors.

✵ ✵ ✵

The dawn came soon after. The mist receded. Erec and Magdalena sat on a stone wall. For a long while, neither spoke. They were exhausted, haunted, and worried.

"This will not relent," said Magdalena quietly. "You realize that."

"Yes," answered Erec. "And it has gotten a whole lot worse."

Magdalena stared up the coast at the castle above them.

"There is only one person who can stop this. And only one person who can stop her."

Magdalena stood. She put her sword in its scabbard.

"I'm going with you," said Erec.

"No, Sir Erec. You find the others. This is something I must do alone."

She faced Erec.

"I have not told you everything about myself. About these isles. I believe Morgause expects me to come to her. But she will not like the outcome of the meeting. She believes I am . . ."

A dark look crossed Magdalena's face. Her weariness was not just from the night's battles. It was something deeper, something in her eyes, in her stillness. She was there and elsewhere at the same time.

Erec observed the Black Knight silently for a moment.

"Listen . . . Mags . . ."

"Don't call me that."

"Oh, right. Sorry."

"Don't ever call me that again."

"Right. Just trying something new. Nickname."

"It's awful."

"I understand."

"I will punch you."

"Got it."

Magdalena nodded to Erec. Erec nodded back.

She left without another word. Erec sat on the wall and watched her go.

CHAPTER TWELVE

GOOD HEARTS

Mel followed Bors across the moors. It was difficult to stay hidden in the flat, treeless terrain once the sun rose. But Mel made good use of rocks and the odd wall. It helped that Bors marched on with furious determination and focus, pausing only occasionally to check a trace or footprint.

He stopped when he reached a craggy outpost some two hundred feet above the thundering surf. Bors took a few cautious steps.

Mel crawled up a rock to get a better view.

The bi-clops—the thing that Sir Hector was now a part of—rested by the opening of a cave.

Mel watched Bors. Bors watched the bi-clops. He was stock-still. And then he drew his sword and strode toward the creature.

Mel leaped up on the stone and drew an arrow.

"Sir Bors!" she yelled.

Bors paused and glanced back at Mel. He narrowed his eyes. Then he drove his sword into the ground.

Without further notice of Mel, Bors approached the bi-clops. The nasty head appeared to be asleep. The Hector head looked at Bors with one sad eye.

Bors sat beside it and put his hand gently on its shoulder.

"Hector, old fellow," Bors said softly, "what have they done to you?"

Mel eased the tension on her bow. She had completely misjudged the situation. She replaced the arrow in the quiver and walked over to Bors and the bi-clops.

"Don't worry, Hector," continued Bors. "I'll get you

out of this somehow. And then we'll make them pay, eh? What do you say?"

The Hector-clops smiled weakly.

Mel stayed a few feet away.

"I heard you a long ways back, Mel," Bors said.

"I thought . . . ," Mel began quietly.

Bors turned.

"Hector's my friend," he said simply.

They sat in silence, except for the roar of the ocean and the snore of the sleeping monstrous side of the bi-clops.

"Hang on, now. One at a time, please."

Erec held his hands up. He was surrounded by villagers. They were not happy.

"Monsters have eaten five of my sheep!"

"They trampled my veg garden!"

"One took our Clive," shouted an old lady. "'Course, I never liked him. . . . ,"

"If you please, have patience," said Erec. "We will rid you of these monsters."

"When?!"

"WHEN?!"

It rose to a chant.

"You knights need to get out!" yelled an old man with one tooth.

"But we're protecting you," said Erec reasonably.

"Protecting us?" scoffed a young lass. "They're after *you*. They only come to the village because you're *here*. If you leave, they will follow."

Everyone quieted down.

"That actually makes sense," admitted Erec. "I hadn't looked at it that way."

"We have!" shouted the villagers.

"Right. Okay. We will take the battle elsewhere," said Erec.

The crowd dispersed with a few last angry looks and muttered words.

Erec took a deep breath. He wandered down the village road. Alone. Where were his companions? What kind of leader was he?

"Sir Erec." Greer stood outside of her home. "I apologize about that."

"They have a point," said Erec.

"Can I show you something?" asked Greer.

She led him into her hovel and over to her shelf of figurines.

"There. On the end," said Greer.

Erec leaned in to get a closer look. There were two new clay figures: one, a skinny wretch with pointy teeth and then, in an action pose, a brave knight.

"Is that me?" asked Erec.

"I'm sorry," said Greer.

"Don't be. This is outstanding work."

"No, that's not what I mean."

A dagger pressed against Erec's throat. Gorp was behind him. Gareth slid from behind a curtain. His sword was drawn and pointed at Greer's back.

"Oh," said Erec, placing the figure back gently.

"They threatened harm to the family next door if I didn't help them," said Greer.

"I understand," said Erec.

"I understand now as well," Greer said.

She turned and spat in Gareth's face.

"You have betrayed your people, Son of Orkney! You call yourself a knight. You are as bad as the monsters!"

Gareth wiped his face slowly. He glared at Greer but then looked away.

"Go, Gorp. Take him," he barked.

"It's that evil queen," said Bors. "She can turn him back."

"No. It was Mordred," said Mel at once. "Mordred and his potion. I'm sure of it."

"Well, let's get the little runt," said Bors.

The sleeping side of the bi-clops stirred. The Hector head shut its eye. Sweat began to appear on its forehead. When the eye opened again, something had changed.

It growled at Bors.

"Hector . . . ," said Bors.

It growled louder and muttered some angry words in

its strange tongue. Then it placed its arm across its eye and held still a moment before pounding itself on the head with its fist.

"He's getting worse," said Mel.

"He's still Hector," said Bors.

The Hector head opened its eye. At the same exact moment, the other head opened its eye.

And its mighty hand shot out and grabbed Bors by the throat.

Mel rolled out of the way as the bi-clops tossed Bors against the rocks. It stood and the monstrous head roared. The Hector head wavered, muttering to itself. Then it too roared.

Bors was back on his feet.

"Fight it, Hector! You're stronger than this! FIGHT!" yelled Bors.

The bi-clops charged Bors. Bors dodged and whacked the monster head with the back of his hand. The bi-clops rounded again and socked Bors on the chin, sending him reeling back toward the edge of the cliff.

Mel's brain ran a mile a minute, calculating their options.

The bi-clops rose up. Both heads were filled with fury. Soon all that would remain of Hector would be the dainty mustache. The bi-clops lifted Bors off the ground, held him high above its heads, and prepared to throw him over the cliff.

Mel put an arrow to her bow, drew the string, and took a breath.

Bors saw Mel poised and ready as he struggled to break free.

"Mel! NO!"

She released the arrow.

It struck the bi-clops on the left side of its chest, beneath the monstrous head. The creature gasped, dropping Bors to the ground. For a moment it wavered, then fell by the rocks.

Bors scrambled over to it. Mel approached slowly, her bow down.

"What have you done?" Bors said hoarsely.

The bi-clops was still. Both eyes were closed.

✿ ✿ ✿

And then . . .

A swirl of purple mist surrounded the creature before blowing away in a gust of wind.

The monster was gone. But the knight was not.

"Hector!" yelled Bors.

Sir Hector stirred, somewhat groggy, then opened his eyes.

"Oh, hello," he whispered.

Mel ran to his side, and she and Bors helped him to a sitting position.

The arrow lay on the ground. Bors picked it up.

"Two heads. Two hearts," said Mel.

"How did you know that?" asked Hector.

"Well . . . it was sort of a guess, really," said Mel.

"Oh. Jolly good," said Hector. "Don't do it again," he added with a smile.

Mel and Bors got Hector to his feet.

"I'll embrace the day when I see the last of this blasted isle," said Bors.

"You're in luck," called a voice.

Gareth stood above them. Gorp held a knife to Erec's throat.

"Today is your last day to see anything."

CHAPTER THIRTEEN

THE SHADOWY ONE

Magdalena approached the castle doors. She stood before them, looking up at the dark keep rising above her. Thick gray clouds blew across the sky. She closed her eyes for a moment, took a breath, and reached for the doors.

They slowly opened of their own accord. No one was inside. The castle was dark, save for a few flickering torches.

The Black Knight entered.

Even though the castle appeared deserted, Magdalena

knew better. She could sense Queen Morgause's presence, feel her eyes watching every move Magdalena made. She entered the throne room. The dais was empty.

The torches guttered, then blazed bright.

Queen Morgause was now seated on her throne.

"Welcome," said the queen.

"I am not here as a guest," said Magdalena. "You know my purpose."

"I most certainly do," said the queen in a low voice. "Your purpose is as clear as the moon and perhaps more ancient."

The queen rose and slowly descended the stairs. Magdalena itched to draw her sword from its sheath, to feel the comfort of its weight and familiarity in her hand, but she remained still.

The queen approached Magdalena.

"How long has it been? How long since you breathed the air of Scotland, felt the moors beneath your feet, drank of the magic in the atmosphere and in the very stones?"

Magdalena was silent.

"You are from Scotland, are you not? From these very isles," said Morgause quietly.

"I was born in Scotland. My parents took me to my father's home in England, where I was raised," said Magdalena.

"Hmm," said the queen. She crossed her chamber and stared out the window at the darkness.

"We have a legend in Scotland," Morgause continued. "Perhaps you have heard it. The Shadowy One, descendant of Scáthach, the greatest warrior in all the world. Her deeds are legend. None could best her in battle. It is said that she will one day return and fight for Scotland."

"I have heard this tale," said Magdalena, not moving a muscle.

"And here *you* are." Morgause turned slowly. "The brave Black Knight. Black. The color of shadows. Interesting."

"I am not your Shadowy One."

A pause.

"You are so certain?" asked Morgause. "Have you looked inside yourself?"

"I know exactly who I am, who I've always been. For a

long time, I hid my identity under a black helmet. Those days are over. I am Magdalena, daughter of Robert the Blacksmith and Fiona of the Isle of Stroma. I serve the good and just King Arthur. I am loyal to his throne and his cause. I am the Black Knight."

"A pity," said Morgause, turning suddenly to walk toward the door.

"You must stop this madness, Queen Morgause. People will die."

"Yes. I'm not surprised that *you* have lasted this long, but I must admit that I am shocked that your fellow knights have survived thus far. No matter. Tonight I will release a horde that will consume this island and all here."

"Including your own sons?"

"Including *all* on this isle. It is for the greater good. The Orkney Isles will stand as the first land of shadow and darkness. The monsters, the nightmares, the legends will spread to England and devour those in my path until I reach Camelot. I shall stand before Arthur and see the fear in his eyes. I will take back what he and his father before him have stolen from my clan."

"No—" began Magdalena, but Morgause was suddenly in front of her, very close.

"Come with me. If not the Shadowy One, then perhaps you could be my . . . Lancelot," she chuckled. "What do you say? Destiny is calling."

The Black Knight drew her sword.

"I do not believe in destiny. I have trained my entire life to become who I am now. And I *shall* stop you."

"Do you know the curse of those who live without destiny, Black Knight?" Morgause smiled sadly. "Unexpected calamity."

Morgause raised her hands into the air and murmured something low. A thick, foul mist rolled across the floor and swirled up the walls. Morgause backed away, into the mist and toward the doors.

The torches burned low.

A stillness filled the great chamber. Then a terrifying noise, like the sound of a million voices whispering and screaming, filled the air.

The mist swirled and twisted and became an enormous, unspeakable thing; a monster of nightmare and doubt and fear and dread.

The chorus of voices rose to a roar.

Magdalena raised her sword and faced the towering monster.

CHAPTER FOURTEEN

AGAIN WITH THE MONSTERS

Gareth tightened the knot. Bors, Hector, Mel, and Erec were all bundled in the cart, their weapons stored out of reach. The worst part of the whole thing was that Gareth hadn't stopped talking for the whole time.

". . . And *then*, then you will know the cunning and strength of the Orkneys!" he crowed.

"Just get it over with already. Untie us and let us battle in a proper manner," said Erec irritably.

Gareth leaned in close.

"Nay. We're taking you to the castle. We have a special room for this. Mordred designed it. It's quite gruesome: dark, dank, filled with chains and—"

"A dungeon," interrupted Bors. "Just say 'dungeon.'"

"It is more than a mere dungeon," called a high, nasally voice.

"Oh, great," muttered Mel.

Mordred appeared by the cart.

"I assure you, you have not seen the likes of our special chamber," Mordred hissed.

"Aye!" shouted Gorp, who, to be honest, the knights had forgotten was standing there, too.

"Yes," continued Gareth, "Arthur's great Band of the Terrible Lizards will fall!"

"And why exactly have they not already fallen?" bellowed another voice. Agravaine rode up on horseback.

"Blimey," complained Erec. "Any more Orkney Boys hiding out in the moors? Could you all get a bit organized, please? I'm getting a neck strain from turning in a new direction every minute or so."

Agravaine dismounted and struck Erec on the mouth.

"Quiet, you. Gareth, explain yourself."

Gareth took a few steps back.

"We did what you said, Agravaine. We thought the monsters would finish them. We just . . . gave them an extra night or two."

"I turned one of them *into* a monster!" boasted Mordred. "But he seems to have gotten better."

"And when that didn't work, we rounded them up to kill back at the castle. Mother will still have their bodies. The plan will still work."

"It had better," said Agravaine. "I have spread the rumor to England, but there is surely still doubt. We must return with their bodies as proof. Then the monsters will invade."

"Oh, right. The monsters," said Erec. "I'm glad you remembered them."

"There's one thing about the monsters . . . ," continued Bors.

"They are very, very . . . ," added Hector.

"Punctual," finished Mel.

All four Orkneys stopped. They looked around. Mist was gathering across the moor. The sun sank below the horizon.

"We are quite good at fighting monsters," said Erec. "How about you Orkneys?"

Agravaine took a step back and drew his sword. The horses whinnied and kicked. Gareth had an ax. Gorp whimpered, holding a club. Mordred crawled under the cart.

All watched the impenetrable mist.

Silence.

Then, with a terrible roar, a horned giant burst out of the gloom, grabbed Gorp, and threw him over a hill.

Gareth and Agravaine attacked and were brushed aside by the giant.

More monsters came. They were all sizes and shapes. Some had flaming heads. Some had no heads at all.

Mordred scrambled out from beneath the cart with a knife in his hand.

Mel laughed.

"Mordred, do you really think you can fight them?"

"No," said Mordred. "But you can."

He sliced the ropes, freeing the knights. In an instant, Mel, Hector, Erec, and Bors were armed and fighting alongside the Orkneys.

The giant spiders turned out to be the worst ones. It took all of the knights, Orkneys, and Mel to defeat them. The entire company ran to the castle, followed by several undead warriors who, although terrifying, were also rather slow. They lost them in no time.

The doors of the castle were smashed off the hinges as they approached. The entire front wall began to crumble, relentlessly pounded from within.

All stood frozen as the colossal, unspeakable horror oozed out of the rubble, tentacles flailing, the din of a thousand screams blasting out.

Mordred stood in rapt wonder. Mel wanted desperately to look away, to find some solace from the feeling of dread that filled her.

The Horror rose to full height and then paused suddenly. The screaming ceased, cut off by a gurgling noise. Then the monstrosity collapsed to the ground.

The blade of a sword sliced out from inside the belly of the beast. The Black Knight emerged, covered in slime but victorious.

Bors chuckled.

"I feel sorry for the monster," he said.

"We have no time," said Magdalena. "Morgause intends to finish all on the island."

She looked at Agravaine.

"Including kin."

"Where did she go?" asked Erec.

"It must be some special place. A source for her magic."

"I know," said Mel and Hector together.

"Eeep," squeaked Mordred.

CHAPTER FIFTEEN

IT TAKES
AN ANGRY VILLAGE

Morgause stood in the center of the circle of stones, her back to the approaching heroes, facing the cliff, the ocean, and the mainland beyond in the darkness.

"Queen Morgause," called Magdalena.

Morgause did not turn. She raised her arms slightly, and the stones began to glow a sickly green light. Mist swirled at her feet, rising slowly from the ground.

"Black Knight. Of course you have survived. I am so very glad. You are not too late to join me."

"We are here to stop you," said Magdalena. "Once and for all."

"'We . . . '" Morgause dragged the word out. She turned to face the company. She smiled.

"You and your fellow Knights of the Round Table. And a child with a bow and arrow. This mighty band against me and the powers of darkness, the shadows and mist, the nightmares and monsters that I have called into our world?"

Morgause laughed.

Agravaine and Gareth stepped out of the darkness by the side of the road. The green glow of the stones danced off their stern faces.

"Well, well, well," said the queen, eyeing her sons. "Now it is getting interesting. My darling sons, have you come to the aid of your mother?"

The Orkney Boys remained silent.

"*Answer me* when I speak to you, wretched children!"

"No," said Agravaine. "We believed that you sought only what was rightfully yours from Arthur. But that is not true, is it? We have seen the ferocity of the creatures you have unleashed. What you seek is mass destruction and murder."

Queen Morgause strode out from within the stone circle and stood before Agravaine.

"You were always slow, Agravaine. However, you are correct. I crave a reckoning. It will be bloody and horrible and complete."

"Mother—"

Morgause held up a single finger to silence him. "You always feared me as a child. Why should that change now?"

Agravaine faltered, looking down.

"Agravaine. Gareth." She spit out their names. "You are as bad as your older brother—my great disappointment—Gawain of *Camelot*. All of you . . . the most wretchedly pathetic offspring any mother has ever been burdened with. You are not worthy to live at my side."

"Mother!" Mordred burst out of the darkness with Gorp.

"Mordred, my darling," whispered Morgause.

"I am loyal, Mother. Always!"

"I know, my little Dreadful. You will always be my true son. But you," Morgause said, looking at Gorp. "I cannot even remember your name."

"Gorp," Gorp whimpered.

Morgause pointed at Gorp and flicked her wrist. Mist engulfed him in an instant, lifted him from the ground, and blew him over the cliff's edge to the sea below.

Agravaine gripped his sword but did not draw it.

Torches flickered in the dark. The villagers surrounded the knights and Mel. Greer stood at the forefront of the mob and pointed at the queen.

"You see! It is true. Queen Morgause brought the monsters to our isle!"

"Of course I have, you ridiculous peasant."

Her arms once again swept up, and the stones burned a bright green. The mist swirled about the villagers, who clung to one another in fear.

"My time in Orkney is at an end. The world awaits,"

continued Morgause. "My dark powers are now beyond—"

"GGGGRRRR!" A hoarse bellow interrupted the queen.

All turned their attention to the circle of stones. Bors was leaning into one of the smaller stones, shoving with all he had. It was beginning to tilt.

"Stop!" yelled Mordred. "Those stones have stood for more than ten years!"

Morgause froze, stunned for the moment. Hector, Mel, and Erec joined Bors in his labor.

Magdalena smiled at the queen, then lent her considerable strength as well. The stone toppled and broke in two. The green light flickered and faded. The mist began to dissipate. The company moved on to the next, this time joined by Agravaine and Gareth.

Queen Morgause hissed. The remaining stones glowed brighter. Shadows moved in from the moors: large, dangerous creatures, their pace increasing. Growls, howls, and roars filled the air.

Greer turned to the villagers. "Come on!"

The men and women of Orkney filled in the circle. They pushed and pushed the stones, working together, despite the mist and the gloom and the terror.

"Push!" called Sir Erec. "PUSH!"

One by one the wretched stones fell until none stood. The mist drifted over the cliff and down to the sea. A hush fell over the darkened moor. The shadows faded as quickly as they had appeared.

Magdalena turned to the queen. "You have lost, Morgause."

"Oh, my dear, misguided warrior, I assure you, I have only just begun."

Morgause snapped her fingers. A galloping sound echoed from the moors. All turned to see a strange white creature fast approaching. It resembled a horse, and yet it was most certainly *not* a horse. Its mane and tail resembled a tangle of seaweed. Its hooves were webbed and clawed. But it was the eyes that most set the creature apart. The eyes of the beast were not at all the kind, thoughtful eyes of a horse. They were the black, empty, remorseless eyes of a shark.

The villagers recoiled, stepping back and huddling close. Several let out screams.

"A nuggle!" cried Mordred, clapping with glee.

"A what now?" said Bors.

Morgause swept onto the nuggle's back and scooped up Mordred to sit behind her. She sneered at Agravaine and Gareth. Then she turned to Magdalena.

"You have chosen poorly, Black Knight."

And with that, Morgause and Mordred rode straight off the cliff.

"Crikey," said Erec.

The nuggle dropped down to the ocean below. It landed on the surface and broke into a gallop, as if the sea were a field of grass. Morgause and Mordred held tight.

A thunder of hooves rang out, and several more nuggles gathered at the cliff in a line, blocking the knights and villagers from pursuit. The nuggles snorted with menace, digging their hooves in the sod.

"Splendid!" cried Sir Erec. "More creepy water horse thingies!"

The knights approached the nuggles.

"Stop!" yelled Greer. "If you mount a nuggle, it will take you to the bottom of the sea. They will drown each and every one of you!"

"Oh," said Erec. He paused.

Then he swung up onto the back of the nearest nuggle. Magdalena, Bors, Hector, and Mel followed suit.

"You are insane," said Greer.

"We are knights. Sanity does not enter into it. We must stop Morgause. These creatures will take us to her," said Erec.

"They will *drown you*," said Greer slowly.

"They will *try*," corrected Magdalena.

"But first they will take us to sea," added Mel.

Agravaine and Gareth also mounted nuggles.

"For Arthur!" shouted Agravaine.

And without another word, the nuggles leaped from the cliff, landed on the ocean's surface, and galloped across the waves, carrying the seven heroes.

The villagers gathered at the edge of the cliff. None spoke. Then Greer smiled and she cheered. All the villagers joined in, raising their pitchforks and torches, filled with something like hope for the first time in many days.

CHAPTER SIXTEEN

A WATERY GRAVE

Far out to sea, surrounded by darkness and the cold, cruel, roiling deep, the heroes spotted Morgause. The nuggles charged across the waves.

"Faster, you monstrous thing," called Erec. "Faster!"

The nuggles did increase their speed, but with each stride they dipped below the surface, beginning their descent to their true destination at the bottom of the sea. They would not reach Morgause in time. It was clear that the nuggles, guided by an ancient and mysterious evil, would indeed take their riders to their drowning deaths.

Bors let out a fierce battle cry. Hector pushed his nuggle to ride faster. Erec grimly set his eyes on Morgause as the waves crashed higher and higher against his steed. Magdalena led the band, determined and unafraid. Agravaine and Gareth drove their nuggles the hardest, fueled by a lifetime of mistreatment and guilt for their role bringing such darkness to the world.

Mel was thinking.

She calculated the distance. She took note of the direction of the wind. She timed the crest of each wave and noticed their frequency.

And then she slipped her bow from her back and pulled an arrow from her quiver. She steadied herself as best she could. Her nuggle had sunk to its belly.

She took aim.

She let the arrow fly.

Mel held her breath as the arrow soared up, up, into the night sky.

She could see the arc of its flight. It would begin its

inevitable descent soon. It would fall short of its mark.

This was the end.

But she would not give up hope. The sea rose to her waist, but still she kept her eyes on the arrow.

And the arrow began to *glow*. It burned bright, as if on fire, and seemed to pick up speed.

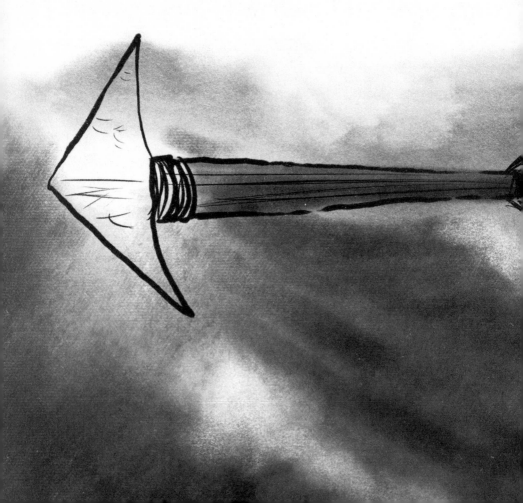

Suddenly a ship appeared from the mist, and there at the prow stood Merlin, his wand raised toward Mel's arrow.

The nuggle dove under the waves. Mel slipped from its back, but the nuggle's seaweed tail wrapped around her leg and dragged her down into the darkness.

A hand grabbed Mel's wrist, and a knife sliced through the seaweed. Magdalena swam upward, pulling Mel to the surface.

Erec, Hector, and Bors swam nearby, also free of their nuggles. Agravaine and Gareth bobbed up to the surface. Merlin's boat sailed alongside the heroes, and there on the deck was Sir Gawain, tossing a fishing net into the sea. All grabbed hold, and Gawain and several others aboard pulled them to safety.

With a final flourish of his wand, Merlin sent Mel's flaming arrow down. It struck Morgause in the shoulder. Wounded, but still astride her nuggle, she halted and turned her steed back. Mordred held tight to her waist. Morgause urged her nuggle in a great circle, faster and faster, creating a vast whirlpool. A column of mist rose from the center and formed a massive cloud that blew toward the mainland.

Merlin turned to the others on the ship.

"Well done, brave heroes. Allow me to take it from here." Merlin caught Mel's eye and held it for a moment.

He gave her a cheerful wink. "I believe this requires a slightly magical touch."

The wizard leaped from the boat. A great whale surfaced and Merlin landed upon its back, riding the whale toward Morgause and the whirlpool.

Mel and the others watched from the deck. The whale and the nuggle faced off, the whale's mighty tail slapping the water and knocking the nuggle over. Morgause and Mordred hung on. Merlin and the whale attacked again. As they fought, both the nuggle and the whale were sucked into the center of the whirlpool. It swirled and churned around them.

Then it stopped. The sea was calm. The thick cloud still drifted toward land. But Merlin, Morgause, and Mordred were gone.

CHAPTER SEVENTEEN

THE DARK AGE

The companions sailed for England immediately and made their way to Camelot as fast as possible. The journey was quiet and tense. Each night brought with it the hint of shadow, a trace of mist, and an overall feeling of unease. No monsters emerged, but the company had no doubt that they were lurking.

Spirits were low. True, Morgause and Mordred were gone, but so was Merlin. A bit of magical power fighting for the side of good would be useful, if not necessary, to vanquish the monsters.

Finally the knights and Mel arrived home. The doors to Camelot opened, and the band entered without fanfare. The castle seemed strangely quiet and empty. They made their way to the chamber of the Round Table.

Bors pushed open the door, and Mel let out a sharp gasp.

"Merlin!"

The wizard sat alone at the table. He was knitting. He looked up as they approached with a smile.

"Scarves are trickier than you would think," he said, indicating the yarn. "Come in, brave knights and courageous archer."

"But we saw you and Morgause—" started Bors.

"You were swallowed by the whirlpool," finished Hector.

Merlin chuckled.

"Oh, it takes more than a whirlpool to end me. However," he added vaguely, "I must keep an eye out for certain trees, apparently. But that's neither here nor there."

"And Queen Morgause?" asked Magdalena.

"Ah, well," said Merlin, packing away his knitting things. "I'm afraid a whirlpool is not enough to defeat Morgause, either. We have not seen the last of her. Or the boy."

The last was mumbled, but Mel heard clearly.

"You mean Mordred?"

Merlin looked up and straight into Mel's eyes.

"Perhaps. One can never know exactly what will happen, can one? People do change. Some for the better."

He rose and patted Mel on the back.

"Cheer up, brave heroes! Don't look so downtrodden."

"But the monsters," said Erec. "We failed to stop them."

"They also failed to stop *you*," said Merlin pointedly.

He paused, then continued.

"And you managed to protect an entire village of innocent people. They know what you did for them. More importantly, they know what *can* be done. There are monsters in our land, creatures of legend and creatures that will become legend. Nightmares that existed in the minds of good people now walk the roads at night. But they can be fought. You have proven that. You, Band of the Terrible Lizards, have *inspired* those people."

"And that is exactly what we need," said a voice from the shadows.

Erec, Bors, Hector, Magdalena, and Mel all knelt as King Arthur joined them at the table.

"Rise, all of you," said Arthur. "There is much to be done."

The company stood before their king.

"A dark age is upon us," continued Arthur. "That is true. Yet we cannot give in to fear. We mustn't give up on hope. We must fight for—and believe in—a better age ahead."

Mel stood a bit taller as Arthur looked in her direction.

"I need—*England* needs—a band dedicated to protecting our citizens from the monsters that are among us," said Arthur. "We need specialists. Given your rather unusual experiences, I can think of no better company."

The band exchanged silent glances.

"We would be honored, King Arthur," said Erec.

"Good."

Arthur and Merlin walked together to the door.

"Besides," Arthur added, "as grail hunters you were complete rubbish."

Merlin cast a final look back. He caught Mel's eye.

"And, archer," said Merlin with a smile, "do let me know if you'd like to learn how to make your arrows a bit more . . . flashy."

And they were gone.

After a moment of reflection, Bors spoke.

"Specialists. I like the sound of that."

"We need a motto," said Hector. "All for one and one for all! No, that's not it . . . but something like that."

"I've no doubt you'll think of something, Hector," said Bors. "And where shall we go first, Erec?"

"Why are you asking me?" asked Erec.

"Well, you're our leader, are you not?"

At first Erec was at a loss for words. "Yes. Thank you, Bors."

"Don't mention it. But you're out as leader if you make any boneheaded decisions," said Bors.

"Absolutely," said Erec with a grin.

Erec turned to Mel.

"You are going to need new arrows, Mel. Lots of them."

"Yes, Sir Erec." Mel beamed.

"Call me Erec."

Magdalena had wandered to the far side of the chamber. She stood by the door, deep in thought.

"And you, Magdalena. What say you?" called Erec.

Magdalena drew her sword and smiled at her companions.

"Let's slay some monsters."

✿ ✿ ✿

Erec, Bors, Magdalena, Hector, and Mel strode out of the hall together. They marched through the great doors of Camelot and down the stone stairs to meet the new day.

They passed the two court minstrels, who paused to admire the company.

"John, my friend, I think we're going to be writing many, many new songs."

A NOTE
FROM
QUEEEN MORGAUSE

I am not surprised that you express interest in learning more about the glorious legends of Scotland and the Orkney Isles. Even the most loathsome of creatures would find our lore irresistibly fascinating. My own disappointing offspring have each devoured these tales with various levels of comprehension. I have included a simple introduction to our many wonders here. The explanations are brief, for I do not know the extent of your intellect. Or worthiness.

I hope—and expect—that this mere taste will inspire you to further explore the rich tapestry of Scottish tradition and legend.

NUGGLES

Nuggles are water spirits found only in the northern islands of Scotland, such as Orkney and Shetland. They resemble horses and are known for luring humans to ride, then dragging them down into deep water.

SCÁTHACH

Scáthach is a legendary Scottish warrior. She is famed for training some of the great heroes of Celtic lore, as well as her own skills in combat and magic. She is said to have lived in an impenetrable castle on the Isle of Skye.

Stone Circles

Circles of standing stones can be seen throughout Scotland, and there are several in Orkney. They are estimated to be around five thousand years old and vary in size. The stone circles may have been used for observing the moon, sun, and stars, or as religious shrines, or as places for social rituals.

As the mysterious vines creep closer to our heroes,
so does their final battle.
What waits at the end of their quest?
Read on for an excerpt from

KNIGHTS
vs.
THE END
(OF *EVERYTHING*)

CHAPTER ONE

SIR GAWAIN & THE GREEN KNIGHT (AND ALSO EREC)

On the last night of the year, a snowstorm engulfed Camelot. Outside the castle, the wind howled, the snow swirled, and the temperature dropped well below freezing.

Inside the castle, the thick stone walls, majestic tapestries, and blazing fires kept out the chill. The brave, good knights of King Arthur's court reveled in the cozy atmosphere, telling stories and jokes, singing songs and toasting good cheer.

✧ ✧ ✧

Until . . .

The great oak doors burst open.

An enormous steed entered the main hall. It was twice the size of a normal horse. Stranger still was its color. It was completely green.

Riding the horse was a giant of a man, regal, strong—and every bit as green as his steed. Silence filled the hall.

The Green Knight dismounted. He held the finest, greenest battle-axe anyone had ever seen.

"Knights of the Round Table," bellowed the Green Knight, "I challenge one of you to take my mighty axe and deal me your finest blow. I shall not defend myself. Use all of your strength, and strike me well and true. Who is brave enough to accept?"

Sir Gawain, noblest of all, rose and stood before the Green Knight. Murmurs peppered the Round Table.

"One more thing," said the Green Knight. "If I survive your blow, in one year's time you must journey to my

castle, where I will have my turn. I shall strike you with all of my might."

Gawain remained silent. Calm. Cool.

"Strike well, brave Gawain." The Green Knight offered his axe, a hint of a smile visible beneath his massive green beard.

Gawain took the axe.

"HOLD IT!" yelled a voice from outside the hall.

Sir Erec strode through the doors, past the green stallion, and right up to the standoff.

"I'll handle this," Erec said casually.

"I say, Erec," said Gawain.

In a flash, Erec took the axe, swung it wide, and sliced the Green Knight's head clean off. The head dropped to the stone floor with a thud. The body remained standing.

A collective gasp sounded from the Round Table.

Erec stepped toward the head.

"Up to your old tricks again, eh?" he said.

Erec gave the head a strong kick.

Another gasp came from the crowd.

The head soared across the hall toward the door, where Sir Bors caught it as he ambled in.

"Unnecessary roughness!" the Green Knight's head roared, his eyes popping open. "Oh, for pity's sake. It's you."

"Hello, froggy!" said Bors with a grin.

"Bors!" grumbled the head. "Release me at once, you rotted stump."

"Gladly." Bors tossed the head over his shoulder. Sir Hector nimbly caught it as he strolled in.

"Tsk, tsk," said Hector. "What are we going to do with you?"

King Arthur rose. "Sir Erec, please explain," he said.

"Yes, Sire," said Erec. "This big lug," he continued, patting the still-standing, headless body, "is a bit of a troublemaker. Nothing we can't handle, of course."

"I, too, could have handled him," said Gawain evenly.

"Quite possibly, Gawain," said Erec. "But we just saved you the bother. The Green Knight is a fairly elaborate prankster. We have experience with him."

"Meddlers, the lot of you!" yelled the green head. "No sense of humor at all. I've never met a worse gang of—"

"Language, Sir Green Knight," said Hector as he turned and lobbed the head into the shadows. The Black Knight entered next, holding it.

"Lady Magdalena!" cried the head. "Present company, excluded, of course. How are you, my dear?"

"Never better," said Magdalena with a smile. "And you?"

"Not bad. I wouldn't mind having my body back."

"Not quite yet," said Erec.

He turned to Arthur.

"My king, we have traveled for the past year. We have fought and defeated many monsters and creatures of the night that Morgause released into the world."

"But . . . ," began Arthur.

"But," Erec continued, "no sign of Morgause herself. Or her son Mordred."

"My mother is very clever, very powerful, and very determined," said Gawain. "Capturing her will not be easy."

"We do not underestimate your mother, Sir Gawain," said Magdalena, joining the others. "We have had too much experience with her for that."

"My brothers Agravaine and Gareth continue their search as well. They were due back in Camelot on the solstice," said Gawain. "But we've had no word from them."

"Perhaps they have found her!" said Hector brightly.

"Wait," said the Green Knight's head. "My mind wandered a bit there. Ha! Joke!"

Bors chuckled. "I get it!"

"But seriously," continued the Green Knight, focusing on Magdalena. "Who are you talking about?"

"Morgause."

"Oh! I've seen her. Calls herself the Queen of Air and Darkness or some such rubbish. Not a pleasant human, that one."

"Where did you see her?" demanded Erec.

"She was visiting her sister. Morgan Le Fay."

Everyone in the hall caught their breath.

Queen Guinevere broke the hush.

"Morgan Le Fay the sorceress?" she whispered.

"The very same, Your Highness," said the Green Knight. "She's practically half-fay nowadays. I suppose that's where she got the name, now that I think about it."

"Can you take us to them?" asked Erec.

"Yes. But you might not like what you find."

The fire crackled. Erec, Hector, Bors, and Magdalena exchanged looks. A year's worth of searching, adventure, horror, and strife were perhaps nearing an end.

"Ahem," coughed the head. "Do you think I could get my body back now?"

Books by
MATT PHELAN

 Greenwillow Books

An Imprint of HarperCollinsPublishers

www.harpercollinschildrens.com